Barbie™

YOU CAN BE A MUSICIAN

by Christy Webster

illustrated by Fernando Güell,
Ferran Rodriguez, and David Güell

Random House 🏠 New York

Barbie loves music.

So does her friend Daisy.

They go to a concert.
Their favorite pop star
is Melody.

"I wish we could
write a song,"
Barbie says.
"Melody can help,"
says Ameera.
She is Melody's manager.

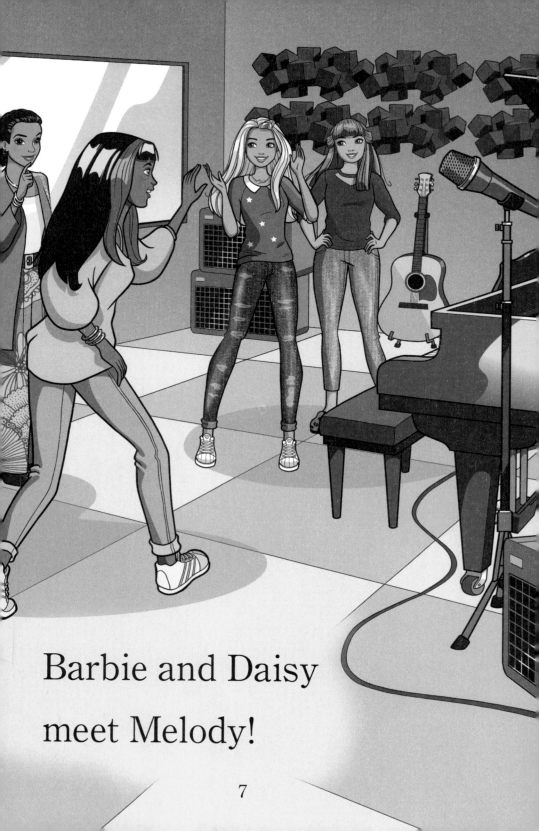

Barbie and Daisy
meet Melody!

Melody tells Barbie
to start with lyrics.
Lyrics are the words
in a song.

Barbie writes down
the words
she wants to sing.

Melody helps Barbie
add music to her words.

She plays piano.

Barbie plays guitar.

They try many ideas.
They work until
they like their new song.

Bradley hears
the new song.

She is a music producer.

She records

Barbie's song.

Bradley shows Barbie
how she records.

First, she records each part.

Then she uses her computer

to mix them together.

Daisy tries the turntable.
She creates a beat
for Barbie's song.

It is time to record!
First, they record
the guitar and
piano music.

Then Barbie enters
the vocal booth.
They will record
her singing.
It is so quiet inside!

Melody helps Barbie
warm up her voice.
They sing high
and low notes.

Barbie puts on headphones.

She hears Daisy's beat.

She hears the guitar
and piano.

She sings the song.

Everyone loves
Barbie's singing!

Bradley shows Daisy
how she mixes the song.
She puts the parts together.
She makes changes.
It sounds great!

Melody has an idea.
Barbie and Daisy
will perform their new
song at her next concert!

Barbie and Daisy
practice all week.

Before the concert,
Barbie and Daisy
rehearse with the band.

The band quickly learns
Barbie's new song.

They play
the song together.
They practice
the song many times.

They want
to be ready
for the concert.

Before the concert,
Daisy is nervous.
"You can do it,"
Barbie says.

Barbie and Daisy
practice one more time.
They are ready!

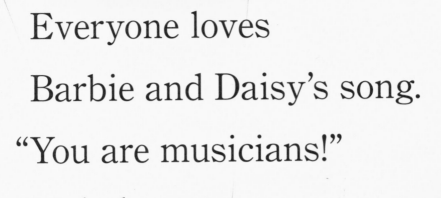

Everyone loves
Barbie and Daisy's song.
"You are musicians!"
Melody says.